# LUCKY CHARMS & BIRTHDAY WISHES

ALSO BY CHRISTINE MCDONNELL

*Don't Be Mad, Ivy*

*Toad Food & Measle Soup*

# LUCKY CHARMS & BIRTHDAY WISHES

by CHRISTINE McDONNELL

PICTURES BY DIANE DE GROAT

*The Viking Press : New York*

First Edition
Text Copyright © 1984 by Christine McDonnell
Illustrations Copyright © 1984 by Diane de Groat
All rights reserved
First published in 1984 by The Viking Press
40 West 23rd Street, New York, New York 10010
Published simultaneously in Canada by Penguin Books Canada Limited
Printed in U.S.A.
1  2  3  4  5  88  87  86  85  84

Library of Congress Cataloging in Publication Data
McDonnell, Christine.   Lucky charms and birthday wishes.
Summary: Emily Mott enjoys the new school
year with a new group of friends.
[1. Schools—Fiction.   2. Friendship—Fiction]
I. De Groat, Diane, ill.   II. Title.
PZ7.M47843Lu   1984      [Fic]      83-19861      ISBN 0-670-44430-8

*For Regina and Jocelyn*

# CONTENTS

# LUCKY CHARMS & BIRTHDAY WISHES

# NEW SEAT, NEW FRIENDS

Emily Mott walked to school slowly on the first day of the new term. It was warm and sunny, too early for the leaves to turn. If it weren't for school, this would have been a good day for swimming. It was still warm enough for shorts, but Emily was wearing a dress. Her mother had asked her to.

"It's nice to dress up a little on the first day of school," Mrs. Mott said. "It celebrates a new beginning."

Emily didn't mind. The dress was sort of a long T-shirt anyway. It didn't itch and it wasn't fussy.

As she walked to school, Emily searched the ground for a lucky charm. A rock with a ring around it, or a very big acorn with a top that could come off like a hat. Maybe a penny. Something she could put in her pencil case and think of as a good-luck charm. It was just a game, but when the familiar brick school came into sight before she had found a charm, she felt a twinge of disappointment.

Her new classroom was on the second floor, with windows overlooking the playground. Mrs. Higgenbottom, her new teacher, sat at her desk giving out name tags.

"Your name, dear?" she asked, giving Emily a warm smile.

"Emily Mott."

Mrs. Higgenbottom handed her a name tag shaped like a ship. "We'll all be explorers to-gether this year," she said.

After each ship had been pinned on to a dress or a shirt, Mrs. H. gave out the seats. "These are just to start with. We might change in a few weeks.''

Emily's desk was the middle desk in the cluster by the window. Ivy Adams sat on one side, and Leo Nolan on the other.

Emily smiled at Ivy, one of those halfway sorts of smiles, the kind that you could pretend wasn't really a smile if the other person didn't smile back. But she didn't have to worry. Ivy Adams grinned back right away. And Leo Nolan smiled when he looked up from the details he was adding to his name tag. He had drawn a cannon on the deck and a pirate symbol on the flag of his ship.

Emily leaned back in her chair and looked around. This was a good seat. It was near the paperback book rack in case she wanted something to read during class. And it was right next to the window. She could see the maple tree across the street, and a large patch of sky.

She wasn't sure about Ivy and Leo, though. She didn't know them very well. Last year she had sat across the room from them both. Leo used to get into trouble, she remembered. And

Ivy was best friends with Phyllis. Emily decided to wait and see. Maybe they would all become friends. Maybe not. You never could tell.

By the end of the first week in school, Emily liked her seat so much that she hoped Mrs. Higgenbottom would forget about changing. Ivy and Leo were friendly and silly.

In other grades Emily had always been very well-behaved in school. She was smart and liked to learn new things. Also, she was a little bit shy, and this made her quiet. A serious child, the teachers used to call her. But you couldn't be serious sitting between Ivy and Leo.

"Hey, Emily, what did the apple say to the grape?" Leo asked.

"I don't know."

"You're very appealing. Get it? A-peeling. Like in apple peel and peel me a grape." Leo was chuckling so hard at his own joke that little tears of laughter spilled out of the corners of his eyes, and he wiped them off with the back of his hand.

Emily smiled, more at his laughter than at

the joke. Ivy laughed. Then all three of them got the giggles together, and that made Leo laugh harder than ever.

Mrs. Higgenbottom gave them a cold look, and they tried to settle down. But it's hard to stop when you've got the giggles. From time to time one of them would let out a snort or a chuckle, and that would start them off again.

Mrs. Higgenbottom gave them another cold look, longer this time. They finally quieted down and went back to doing their arithmetic sheets.

Emily felt a hum of pleasure inside. Teachers had never given her cold looks before. They always used to send beams of approval her way, making her feel set apart just because she knew the right answer. But now she was included along with Ivy and Leo. She was part of them. It was nice to be in trouble for a change, if you were in trouble together. This was going to be a good year, Emily decided.

On her way to school the next week Emily found the lucky charm she had been looking for. It was a smooth flat oval rock, smoke-gray, with a thin white stripe circling it. It was exactly the right size; it fit in the center of her palm. She tucked it in her pocket, and when she got to class, she put it in her pencil case.

Ivy saw her.

"What's that?"

"A rock I found on my way to school."

"Why're you putting it in there?"

Emily hesitated. She didn't want Ivy to think she was silly. But everybody knew that rocks with stripes around them are lucky.

"It's a lucky charm. It has the stripe around it."

She handed it to Ivy.

"Is it really lucky?" Ivy asked.

Emily nodded. "Every stone with a stripe that goes completely around it is lucky. My father told me."

Ivy examined the rock, running her fingers over its cool surface and tracing the white band.

"Do you think I could find one?"

"Sure, if you look carefully."

Ivy looked all week but couldn't find one. Leo was looking for one, too. By Friday they were both discouraged.

"Guess we just aren't lucky," said Leo.

Emily tried to cheer them up. "You don't really need a stone to be lucky."

"Well, it sure might help," said Ivy.

All day Friday Emily worried. Maybe Leo and Ivy won't like me because of this, she thought. I wish I had never found the lucky stone. Maybe it's a bad-luck charm, not a good-luck charm.

That afternoon the class had a spelling test. Ivy and Leo each missed one word. Emily got every one right.

"See," said Ivy. "It does help to have a lucky charm."

Leo nodded.

Emily didn't really think that the stone had anything to do with getting one hundred on the test. She had always been a good speller. But she didn't want to argue about it. She just wanted to be friends.

On Saturday Emily went to visit her Grandmother Eve. After lunch they went for a walk on the beach near her grandmother's house. The sun made the sand glint, and the wind made whitecaps on the waves. They walked quietly together, Grandma looking for sea glass and shells, Emily searching for lucky stones.

"Gran, are lucky stones lucky if you don't find them yourself?" Emily asked.

Grandma thought about it for a minute. Emily could tell she was thinking because she made a tiny wrinkle between her eyebrows, and she pushed her hands deep into the pockets of her corduroy pants.

"I think a lucky stone can bring you luck if the person who gives it to you is your friend and truly wants you to be lucky."

Emily listened carefully, then kept on searching for stones with rings around them. Near the jetty she found a little white one with a band of black, and just below the steps that led up to her grandmother's house, she found a speckled stone with a white stripe around it. She placed both of them carefully in her pocket.

On Monday Emily gave the little white stone to Ivy and the speckled one to Leo. They were surprised and pleased.

*11:*

"Hey, thanks!" said Ivy. "I really wanted this."

"Me too," said Leo. "Now we're like a team. We should call ourselves The Lucky Stones."

"Let's click our stones together for luck," said Ivy.

Emily got hers out of her pencil case.

"Friends for the year," said Leo, knocking his stone against Emily's and Ivy's.

"Friends for the year," said Emily and Ivy, tapping their stones together.

Emily smiled to herself. She felt both lucky and happy. This was going to be a good year. She was sure of it.

# THE ORIGAMI TRUCE

Every day in September at recess Emily and Ivy liked to play games with the small pink balls you could buy at the candy store, the ones called high bouncers. Their friends played, too.

"A my name is Alice and my husband's name is Arthur and we live in Alabama and we sell anteaters."

Phyllis bounced the ball in a steady rhythm, swinging her leg over every time she said an A word. Then she went on to the B's.

"B my name is Barbara and my husband's name is Bill and we live in Boston and we sell barracudas." She was trying to think of an animal for every letter in the alphabet.

Emily stood next to Patricia O'Hare, waiting for her turn. Phyllis missed on the letter E. She couldn't think of an E place.

"Egypt," suggested Emily. She always knew E because that was the letter that her own name began with.

The next one up was Patricia. Her bushy curls bounced in rhythm with the ball. She went through the letters quickly. But at J she couldn't think of something to sell. She gave the ball an angry bounce before she tossed it to Emily.

Emily had got up to the letter G when something hard hit her on the back of her neck, making her miss her next bounce.

She rubbed her neck where it stung and looked around. Not far from the circle of girls stood Johnny Ringer, grinning.

"What's the matter, Mott? Can't even bounce a ball?"

"I was doing fine until you came along."

Johnny laughed. "Made you miss, huh?"

"Yeah, you made me miss."

"See. You're not perfect, after all."

"I never said I was."

"Think you're so smart. Showoff."

Emily felt herself blush. Johnny wasn't being fair. She wasn't a showoff.

"Get lost, Ringer," said Ivy. "Find a cliff and jump off."

"Yeah," said Patricia. "You think you're so tough."

"Johnny is a je-rk, Johnny is a je-rk," Phyllis chanted.

Emily didn't say anything. She looked down at the playground and kicked a pebble away. It was probably the same pebble that Johnny had thrown.

"Ah, what do you know, anyway?" said Johnny. He sauntered off with his hands in his pockets, trying to walk like a tough guy.

From that point on, Johnny Ringer picked on Emily at least twice a week. He put paste on her chair. He stole her spelling notebook and hid it behind the hamster cage. He wrote on her desk with a Magic Marker, ''Emily Mott Is a Snot,'' and it wouldn't wash off.

''I don't get it,'' Ivy said. ''What did you ever do to him?''

Emily shrugged. She didn't know.

Finally Leo took Johnny aside. ''Listen, Ringer, you're acting dumb. Emily hasn't done anything to you.''

''How do you know?''

''Name one thing she's done.''

''She gives me a pain. She thinks she's so smart, always winning the math relays and stuff.''

Leo shook his head. ''That's dumb.''

''Don't call me dumb. I'm sick of people calling me that.''

''Okay. But listen. Leave Emily alone.''

''What'll you do if I don't?''

''You'll find out,'' said Leo in a low voice.

Johnny looked at him carefully but said nothing. Then, with a quick dart of his fist, he punched Leo in the arm and stepped away fast.

Leo rubbed his arm and went back to his desk.

Emily looked up.

"What a jerk," Leo said, still rubbing his arm. "He doesn't like you because you're smart, Emily."

Emily brushed her bangs out of her eyes and straightened her glasses. "What?"

"That's what he said." Leo made a silly face, as if to try to cheer her up.

Emily looked across the room. Johnny stood by the hamster cage, poking his pencil between the bars.

After that, Emily tried to keep a distance between herself and Johnny. She sat far away from him at lunch and at singing. She wasn't in his reading group, and she hoped she'd never be paired with him in math. At recess she stuck with the other kids, figuring that he wouldn't bother her if she was part of a group.

Ivy tried to cheer her up. "Maybe he'll find someone else to pick on. Maybe he'll catch chicken pox or get the flu and stay out of school for a month. Maybe he'll move away."

Her ideas made Emily smile, but inside she was still worried.

Emily even tried to hide being smart a little. She stopped raising her hand when she knew the answer, and sometimes she made mistakes on purpose when she was at the blackboard.

"Emily, that isn't like you," said Mrs. Higgenbottom. "What's the matter, dear?"

She looked so concerned that Emily almost blurted out the whole problem. But she stopped herself just in time. What could Mrs. Higgenbottom do about it, anyway? Besides, if Johnny found out, he might do something terrible. Maybe he would get hold of her cat and torture it, or something even worse. So she didn't tell Mrs. Higgenbottom, after all.

One day at the beginning of October Mrs. Higgenbottom told the class, "We're having a visitor with us for a few weeks, a teacher from another country. His name is Mr. Uchida, and he's from Japan."

Everyone began to talk at once.

"Can he speak English?"

"What does he look like?"

"What do they eat in Japan?"

"When's he coming?"

The questions blurred together in a hubbub.

"Class, simmer down. I'll answer your questions one at a time."

Mrs. Higgenbottom showed them where Japan was on the globe, and she propped a big map of Japan against the board. The class spent the rest of the afternoon making lists of questions to ask Mr. Uchida.

He arrived on Monday. He had gray hair and a very soft voice. He showed them slides of his town and of the children at the school where he taught.

Every day the class learned something new about Japan. Sometimes they pushed all the desks away and sat on straw mats. They practiced eating with chopsticks, and they learned Japanese words.

Emily was disappointed by some of the things that Mr. Uchida told them. Japanese cities looked a lot like American cities—big, modern, and crowded. People wore the same kinds of clothes as they did in America—suits and dresses and even blue jeans.

"But there are some things that are very

different,'' Mr. Uchida assured them, and he showed them colorful kimonos and wooden clogs. He taught them how to draw with black sumi ink and brushes, and how to write short poems called haiku. You had to count the syllables, five in the first line, then seven, then five in the last line. Each poem was like a puzzle; you had to search for the right-size words.

Emily wrote a haiku about Johnny:

> *Like a big mean dog*
> *he chases me all around*
> *biting at my heels.*

Then she tried another:

> *Is he really mad*
> *because I know the answers,*
> *or is he jealous?*

She wrote haiku about Leo and Ivy:

> *He's a funny clown*
> *who wears a smile and a joke.*
> *My friend cheers me up.*

*She's a bouncing ball.*
*She likes to talk, laugh, and play.*
*She sticks up for me.*

Emily had so much fun writing haiku that she didn't worry about Johnny for a while. But when Mr. Uchida put her haiku up on the board with her sumi ink pictures, she saw Johnny glare at her again.

After Mr. Uchida had been with the class for two weeks, he arrived one afternoon with a basket full of colored paper.

"Today we will begin to learn origami, the art of paper folding."

One by one, he held up tiny figures of birds and animals made out of paper. There was a penguin, a frog, and a crane that even flapped its wings.

Everyone got several sheets of paper. Emily picked green, blue, yellow, and a deep rose. Ivy picked pink and purple, black and brown.

"I want to make a bear," she said.

Mr. Uchida taught them how to make the first basic folds. Then he gave out instruction

*21:*

sheets for three easy figures—a house, a boat, and a cup.

The first person to finish all three was Johnny Ringer. Mr. Uchida examined his figures.

"Very well done," he said, and pinned them up on the bulletin board. "You may take a more difficult sheet now. You will use the same basic folds, but the figure is more complicated. Follow the directions carefully."

Johnny picked out the penguin sheet. He made the figure out of black paper. Mr. Uchida showed him how to turn the corners into flippers, and how to shape the head and the bill. Johnny's penguin came out perfectly on the very first try.

"You are very good at this, my friend," Mr. Uchida complimented Johnny. "Let me see your hands."

Johnny held out his hands cautiously. He wasn't sure what Mr. Uchida was looking for. Both hands were grimy, with dirt under the fingernails and around the knuckles. There were spots of ink and red Magic Marker, but Mr. Uchida didn't seem to notice.

"Look how long and tapered your fingers are. You have very smart fingers, Johnny."

Johnny looked down at his hands, admiring them.

Mr. Uchida patted him on the shoulder. "Take care of those hands. They are a sign of special talent."

Johnny blushed. For once he had nothing to say. He just smiled quietly and picked another sheet.

From then on, Johnny was the expert at origami. His figures were always the best. His folds were straight. He was careful and patient. He moved quickly but never hurried. Soon he became Mr. Uchida's helper, showing the others how to turn a fold inside out, or how to line up the edges exactly. The bulletin board was covered with Johnny's paper animals.

Emily was just no good at origami. She couldn't get the folds right. She couldn't line up the corners, and she couldn't understand the instructions. Her little figures were wrinkled and dirty from the sweat of her fingers. The harder she tried, the more frustrated she became. But she wouldn't give up. She wanted to learn how to make the crane, the graceful little figure that could flap its wings.

She tried and tried. Once, when she looked up, Johnny was watching her. He wasn't laughing. He looked as if he knew just how she felt. Emily quickly looked down at her work again. She felt stupid and clumsy. On purpose, she crumpled a sheet of origami paper into a ball and threw it angrily on the floor. The next time she picked a fresh sheet of paper, Johnny came over to her desk.

He showed her how to line up the corners before making the folds.

"Go slow. Don't rush," he said.

His fingers moved smoothly. Emily followed him, step by step.

"Now I get it!" she said.

Johnny left her on her own, and she finished making the frog and started on the penguin.

That afternoon when she caught Johnny's eye on the playground, he smiled at her instead of glaring or making a face. She waved back.

Soon it was the last week of Mr. Uchida's

visit. Emily tried to work up to doing the crane. She got stuck on the bear for a day, and she still had a hard time making the long diamond shape that was the base for the crane.

"I'll never get it done," she complained to Ivy.

"So? You can keep on trying after he leaves."

"No. We'll go on to something new. I know it. It's now or never."

She kept on trying.

On Thursday Mr. Uchida wasn't at school.

"This gives us a chance to get ready for Mr. Uchida's good-bye party tomorrow. We have all day to prepare our surprise," said Mrs. Higgenbottom. "What should we make for him?"

"Let's make good-bye cards with sumi ink," said Ivy.

"And write haiku," said Emily.

"Let's make him a paper kimono to wear at the party," suggested Mary Louise. "We can paint it with birds and flowers to make it look like silk."

Emily looked across the room. Everyone was

talking and making plans. Everyone except Johnny. He sat by himself in the reading corner staring out the window.

Poor Johnny, Emily thought. He's going to miss Mr. Uchida. She sat for a while chewing on her pencil and thinking. Then she raised her hand.

Mrs. Higgenbottom nodded. "What is it, Emily?"

"I think we should decorate the room with origami. All different colors. We can hang them on strings, lots of them, by the windows and in front of the boards and from the lights, too."

"Hey, that'll look great," Ivy said.

Mrs. Higgenbottom agreed. "Good idea. But who will make them all? We haven't much time."

"Johnny!" shouted the class.

Johnny looked up, surprised.

"How about it, Ringer?" called Leo.

"Okay," said Johnny. "I guess I can do it."

They spent the day preparing for the party. Emily wrote haiku. Ivy drew pictures. Leo and Phyllis practiced a puppet show. Mary

Louise and Patricia worked on the kimono. And Johnny sat by the window and made origami figures. The class stopped their projects after lunch to learn a Japanese song, and they each wrote a letter to a child in Mr. Uchida's class in Japan.

"I hope they write back," said Leo.

Johnny wrote an extra letter. The envelope said, "To Mr. Uchida." Emily noticed it when she put her letter in the box.

"Want some help hanging up your animals?" Emily asked Johnny.

He nodded. "But be careful not to bend them."

They strung the figures across the boards and hung them in front of the windows. The wind turned them gently on their threads.

"They look like they're flying," Emily said.

They finished just before the bell rang for the end of school. The room was cleared, with desks pushed against the back wall. The floor was covered with mats, and a few pillows from the reading corner were set out.

"Tomorrow everyone should bring in a pillow to sit on. And remember to take off your shoes outside the room,'' Mrs. Higgenbottom reminded them. ''And, Johnny, be sure to be here a little early. You'll be the class host for the day because you've been Mr. Uchida's special assistant.''

Johnny stood up very straight and nodded.

The party on Friday was a great success. Mr. Uchida smiled and clapped at everything. He laughed at the play, admired the paintings, and read every poem out loud.

''My students will enjoy getting your letters, and they will write to you in return, I promise.''

When it was time to leave, Mr. Uchida put his arm around Johnny.

''Good-bye, special assistant. You've been a big help. Don't forget to take care of those hands, and write to me sometime.''

Johnny nodded, but he couldn't smile.

Mr. Uchida seemed to understand. He gave him a pat on the head.

Mr. Uchida left after lunch, and the class put the room back in order. Emily watched

Johnny carefully take down his little origami figures. He still looked sad.

I wonder what he's going to do with all those, she thought. She wanted to ask him, but she was a little bit afraid. She remembered how he used to tease her.

But that had been before Mr. Uchida came.

Trying to feel brave, Emily went over to the board where Johnny was working.

"Johnny?"

He looked up.

"What are you going to do with your little animals?"

He shrugged.

"I was wondering." She paused, then started again. "I was hoping that maybe you'd give me one of your cranes. I never managed to make one, and I really wanted to. I could use yours for a model."

A big smile spread across Johnny's face. "Sure. I'll pick you out the best."

As the bell rang that afternoon, Johnny gave Emily a perfect crane made out of deep blue paper. He left quickly. She only had time to say, "Thanks," as he disappeared out the door.

She examined the little figure carefully. Each fold was perfect. She could imagine it flying over the water. She was about to tuck it between the pages of her library book for safekeeping on the trip home when she noticed some writing on the underside of the wings.

She turned it over and read the tiny printing: "For Emily from your friend, Johnny."

She put it carefully in her library book. Then she took one of her haiku and sumi ink paintings from her desk, and on the back she wrote, "For Johnny from your friend, Emily." She put it carefully inside Johnny's desk.

Then she whistled happily all the way home.

# LYDIA

The house next door to Emily's had dark brown shingles and two tall stone chimneys, one at each end. A thick grove of trees surrounded it, and a wooden fence separated it from the houses on either side. Hidden by the trees, the house seemed scary. It was different from the others on the block, with their wide-open lawns and clipped hedges. The Witches' House, the children called it, and dared each other to climb the fence and walk through the woods alone.

Emily knew it wasn't a witches' house, even though she liked to pretend that it was. Mrs. Steele lived there with her sister, Miss Lacy. They were smiling gray-haired ladies who liked to work in the garden and borrowed armloads of books from the library each week. Mrs. Mott, Emily's mother, often climbed over the fence and took a shortcut through the woods to trade books and drink coffee with them. In the summer Miss Lacy brought over bags of zucchini and tomatoes from their garden.

Because only grownups lived in the Witches' House, the children on the block seldom went there, except to sell Girl Scout cookies or raffle tickets for the Little League. Miss Lacy and Mrs. Steele always waved when they drove past in their old green car. But the children felt shy around them. Besides, it was more exciting to pretend that witches lived in the old house.

In the middle of December Emily's mother got a telephone call from Mrs. Steele.

"My niece, Lydia, is coming for the holidays," she said. "Her father is in the hospital, and her mother's got so much on her mind that she won't have time for a real Christmas. So Lydia's coming to stay with us. It's always fun to have a child in the house at Christmas.''

Mrs. Mott agreed.

''Lydia's just Emily's age. Do you think Emily would like to come over on Friday afternoon and get acquainted?''

''Certainly,'' said Mrs. Mott.

So on Friday Emily walked around the edge of the woods until she reached the stone gateposts that stood at the front of the driveway. She turned in and walked up to the house.

Lydia's a funny name, Emily thought as she knocked and waited on the doorstep. Old-fashioned, like a name in a book. A name for an orphan or a little girl who lives on a farm.

Just then Mrs. Steele opened the door. ''Come in. I'm so glad to see you. Emily, this is my niece, Lydia. Lydia, this is Emily Mott, who lives next door.''

Emily smiled, feeling a little shy. Lydia had dark brown hair in two long braids and bangs that hid her eyebrows.

"Why don't you two go play and get to know each other?" said Mrs. Steele, taking Emily's coat.

Emily followed Lydia through the living room to a sun porch with window seats. A fire burned in the fireplace.

"Want to play checkers?" asked Lydia. She sounded just as shy as Emily felt.

They sat cross-legged on the window seat with the board on the cushion between them. Emily won one game and Lydia won two. Then they played a few rounds of Fox and Geese. It was easier to win if you were the geese, so they traded sides every game. Emily won once when she was the fox.

As they played, they talked. They found out that they were in the same grade, but Lydia was two months older. They both liked to read. Lydia had just finished the Narnia books, and Emily was right in the middle of *The Lion, the Witch, and the Wardrobe*. Before they knew it, it was time for Emily to go home.

"Can you come over tomorrow?" Lydia asked. "We can go up in the attic. Aunt Alice says there's trunks of old clothes and maybe some old toys, too.''

Emily waved good-bye and ran down the driveway. At the gatepost she looked back at the house. Even in the twilight it didn't look scary anymore. Lydia stood at the window, waving.

''She's exactly my age almost, and she has long hair way past her shoulders,'' Emily told her parents at dinner. ''And we both like to read. I'm going back tomorrow.''

''Looks like this visit is going to be a success,'' said Mrs. Mott.

The next morning the sky looked gray and heavy.

''Snow by noon,'' Mr. Mott predicted.

After breakfast Emily went next door. She climbed the fence this time and took the short-cut through the woods. Lydia was waiting at the front door.

''I saw your red hat coming through the trees,'' she said.

Emily pulled off her mittens and her jacket and rubbed her hands together. ''My father says it's going to snow.''

"I hope so," said Lydia. "We could go sledding. Hey, look!" Lydia pointed out the window. "It's started!"

Fat white flakes were beginning to gather on top of the cold ground.

"I hope it keeps up all day," said Emily.

"Come on up to the attic," Lydia said. "I want to explore."

She led the way up the wood-paneled staircase. Past the second-floor landing the stairs were steep and narrow. The air had a dry, sweet smell.

Emily sniffed. It reminded her of the lavender her grandmother tucked away with the sheets.

In the front room of the attic they found three wooden trunks with curved lids and bands of tarnished metal. The first thing Lydia pulled out was a flat black circle, stiff and thick.

"It's a top hat," she said. "Watch."

She bent the brim just a little and—POP!— up came the hat, tall and shiny.

"It's a snowman's hat," said Emily. "Maybe we can use it later, outside."

Next there were two dresses made of stiff,

smooth material. Lydia handed the blue one to Emily and stepped into the red one herself, pulling it on right over her jeans. The skirt covered her sneakers and dragged along the floor. Emily pulled on the blue dress.

"We need a mirror," Lydia said. She went to look in the next room. "Come on in here," she called.

Leaning against the wall was a tall mirror, its wooden frame carved with flowers and vines. The glass was speckled and gray in places. Emily and Lydia stood side by side in front of it. In the mirror's dim reflection stood two girls from long ago, one blond, the other dark-haired. They matched the old mirror perfectly, like a moment frozen from the past.

Silently the girls gazed at themselves. Then Emily whispered, very low, so as not to break the spell, "This is the way our great-grandmothers looked, I bet."

Lydia nodded. She stared at the girl in the mirror as if she were trying to know her better. Then she noticed something else in the mirror.

"What's that?" she said.

It looked like an old house, over by the wall.

Both girls turned quickly. It was a big doll-house, its roof almost as high as their waists.

"We need a light," Lydia said. "I'll go get one from Aunt May." She rustled off, leaving Emily alone in the room.

Emily knelt in front of the dollhouse and looked closely. It was covered with brown shingles, with a chimney at each end. The little windows had diamond-shaped panes of glass.

It's old, she thought. Maybe it belonged to the girl who wore this dress.

She touched the front door carefully with one finger. It had a little doorknob and a tiny knocker. Then she leaned back on her heels and took another look. Somehow the house looked familiar.

That's impossible, she thought. I've never seen it before. Maybe I saw one like it in a book or at the museum.

She couldn't shake off the feeling that she had seen it before. Then, in a flash, she knew.

It was the Witches' House, the house she was sitting in right this second. It was a dollhouse model of this very same house!

When Lydia reappeared with a big blue lamp, Emily showed her the similarities. The lamp helped the girls see the tiny latches that held the front of the dollhouse in place. They lifted it off carefully and pushed back the hinged roof.

"The inside's exactly the same, too," said Lydia.

There was the hallway, with the living room and the sun porch off to one side and the dining room and kitchen off to the other. The curving staircase went up to the second floor, with bedrooms and a funny little bathroom that even had an old-fashioned claw-footed bathtub.

Very carefully the girls examined the house. In every room there was old-fashioned furniture. In the nursery there were even old-fashioned toys: a little rocking horse, a wagon, and a tiny toy house.

"A dollhouse inside a dollhouse," said Lydia.

"Maybe there's a dollhouse inside the dollhouse inside the dollhouse," Emily joked. "Just like those books that have a picture of the boy reading the same book with the same picture on the cover. And if you look, you can see that the book on the cover of his book has the same picture, too. And it keeps on going, getting tinier and tinier.''

''There aren't any people,'' Lydia said. ''Everything else is here except the people. They should be here, too.''

''Maybe they got lost. Or broken,'' said Emily. ''Or maybe somebody packed them away.''

Lydia searched the house once more, trying to find the dolls. ''They're not here.''

''We could make some. We could use clothespins or pipe cleaners and felt and stuff.''

''It wouldn't be the same. They wouldn't look old enough,'' Lydia said. ''Let's go ask my aunts. Maybe they know where they are.''

Miss Lacy and Mrs. Steele were sitting in the sun porch. One was reading and the other was knitting. They had a fire burning in the fireplace again. Outside, the snow swirled by the windows in white gusts, and the ground was completely covered. It looked as if several inches of snow had fallen already.

''My, don't you look fine!'' said Miss Lacy.

"Those dresses belonged to your great-grand-mother, Lydia. They suit you two very well."

"We found them in the trunk," Lydia said, "and we found an old dollhouse, too. It's exactly like this house. All the windows, the staircases, everything! It's perfect, except there aren't any people. Do you know where they are? Whose house was it, anyway? It looks so old."

"Questions, questions!" Mrs. Steele laughed. "Yes, it's very old. It was here when we were children. The carpenter who built this house took a liking to your great-grandmother. She was only a little thing, no more than five years old, I think. Anyway, he built her the dollhouse exactly like the big house."

"So it did belong to the girl who wore this dress," said Emily.

"That's right," said Mrs. Steele. "In the pictures she looks something like you, dear. She had blond hair like yours."

"But what about the people? There must have been doll people who lived in the house," Lydia interrupted.

"Do you remember the dolls, May?" Mrs.

Steele asked Miss Lacy. "I recall there was a whole family."

Miss Lacy took off her reading glasses and thought for a moment. "Yes, I remember them. There was a mother and a father. The father wore glasses. And there were a sister and brother and a wonderful soft little baby. And there was a cook, all dressed in white."

"I always thought she was the nursemaid," said Mrs. Steele.

"Oh, no, she was the cook. There was lots of food, too. Hard painted food. Meat on a platter, and little fruits, and pies. Remember?"

The two gray-haired sisters smiled at each other, remembering the dollhouse as it was when they were young.

"Isn't this fun, having the house come to life again!" said Miss Lacy. She smiled at the girls. "It's almost as if you were us and we were you somehow!"

"But where are the dolls?" Lydia said impatiently. "They're not in the dollhouse."

"Where could they be if they're not in the house?" Miss Lacy wondered. "Maybe your mother would know. She played with them when she was little, and that was years after we did. We were almost grown when she came along. Maybe she put them away somewhere. We'll ask her tonight when we call.''

After lunch Emily and Lydia did not go back upstairs to play. They went outside instead and made a snow family on Emily's lawn. The father wore the top hat from the attic. The mother wore an old shawl that Mrs. Mott lent them. The children wore woolen hats that Emily found on the coatrack by the kitchen door. It was still snowing when they finished.

''See you tomorrow,'' called Lydia as she started to trudge back to the big brown house in the woods. ''Maybe we'll find the dolls.''

''I hope so,'' called Emily, waving good-bye.

# THE DOLLHOUSE CHRISTMAS

Lydia knocked on the Motts' kitchen door soon after breakfast the next morning.

"Can you come over?" she asked Emily.

"I'd like you two to play outside for a while again today," Mrs. Mott said, looking up from her second cup of coffee. "It looks beautiful out there with the sun and the fresh snow."

Emily nodded. "We'll go sledding this afternoon. We promise." That gave them the whole morning to play in the attic.

Emily pulled on her boots and jacket and then followed Lydia through the trees. The snow was almost up to her knees.

"Did you find the dollhouse people?" Emily asked.

Lydia nodded, her bangs flopping beneath her knitted hat. "My mother told me last night on the phone. We never would've found them."

"Were they somewhere else in the attic?"

"No! They were in the closet of my room. It used to be my mother's room when she was little. The dollhouse used to be in there. It only got moved upstairs after she grew up."

"They were in the closet?"

"Yes. In a cigar box on the top shelf. My mother put them all away together, wrapped in tissue paper, the whole family."

Emily couldn't wait to see them. "Where are they now?"

"I put them in the dollhouse. Come on upstairs. You can see for yourself."

The attic gleamed with light reflected off the snow on the roof. Emily knelt in front of the dollhouse, straightened her glasses, and peered in.

The whole family was there. The mother and father sat in the living room. The father was holding a tiny newspaper. The mother sat at the piano with her hands on the keys. The cook was in the kitchen standing in front of the stove. The children were in the nursery. The boy sat on the rocking horse, the girl stood in front of the window, and in the wooden cradle lay the baby.

Emily held her breath for a second. It all looked so real! Everyone fit perfectly in the rooms. It looked like a picture from an old-fashioned book, all proper and settled.

"Wait till you look at their clothes," Lydia said. She reached in and roughly grabbed the father doll.

Emily winced for him. "Be careful. He's old," she said. It wasn't just that he was old. He looked dignified. It didn't seem right to pick him up just any old way.

Emily carefully lifted up the other dolls and examined their clothes and their faces.

Each had a different expression.

"They look like real people," she said.

Lydia looked at the father's face as if she were seeing him through Emily's eyes. "You're right, he does look real. He looks serious but nice, especially with his glasses. You think he's going to be strict, but he isn't."

She put him back in the living room armchair and set the newspaper in front of him again.

"They need names," said Emily. "Did your mother remember their names?"

"She said we should name them ourselves. Do you have any ideas?"

Emily studied the family. "I think their last name is Higgins. Mr. and Mrs. Higgins."

Lydia tried it out. "Higgins. Sounds good. I want to name the girl."

"You should name the boy, too. It's really your family."

"Okay. You can name the baby and the cook."

They each sat on the floor with the dolls they were naming in their laps.

These are better than ordinary dolls, Emily

thought. They have real faces. It's as if they're a real family.

"The girl's name is Martha, and the boy's name is William," Lydia announced. "Martha's nickname is Marty. William doesn't have a nickname."

"The cook is Mrs. Cress, but the family calls her Hilda," Emily decided. "And the baby is named May, because that's the month she was born in."

"Marty, William, and Baby May." Lydia repeated the names out loud. "And Mr. and Mrs. Higgins and Hilda, the cook with the terrible temper."

"Children, chil-dren! Get out of my kitchen this minute. Can't you see I'm making pie? Haven't got time for you two now. Scoot! Go on, scoot!" Emily pretended to be Hilda.

"We want to help. Let us help. We can make the pie crust," said Lydia, pretending to be Marty.

"No, no, *no*!" said Hilda the cook. "Go along with you. Upstairs and play. The kitchen is no place for you."

## The Dollhouse Christmas

The girls played with the dollhouse family all morning. It was almost noon when they realized they were hungry. They went next door for lunch.

"You two promised to play outside, remember?" Mrs. Mott reminded them when they came in.

So after tomato soup and grilled cheese sandwiches the girls walked down to the railroad station, dragging sleds behind them.

The hill was long and steep, with one big bump right in the middle. Off to the side was a little hill that the younger children used.

Emily recognized Ivy by her striped ski hat. She waved, and Ivy ran over, taking giant steps through the snow.

"This is Lydia. She's staying next door at her aunts' for Christmas," Emily told Ivy.

"Good! Then you can come caroling with us tomorrow," Ivy said.

"We all go every year," Emily explained. "You can come with my family. We carry candles, and afterwards we drink hot cider."

"I'll ask my aunts," Lydia promised.

*51:*

The next day Emily didn't have time to play with the dollhouse at all. She helped her father pick out the Christmas tree in the morning, at the lot behind the fire station. Then, in the afternoon, the telephone rang. It was Mrs. Steele calling Mrs. Mott.

"Lydia's excited about caroling tonight. But I wanted you to know that she's also quite worried about her father. His condition hasn't improved. Lydia knows that it's serious. We appreciate everything you're doing to cheer her up."

"Why don't you send her over right now?" Mrs. Mott suggested. "We're making cookies and then we'll decorate the tree. In fact, why don't all three of you come over? We'd love to have you."

"Oh, we couldn't impose. Christmas is for family."

"Nonsense! It will be more fun if you come. The more the merrier."

Mrs. Mott persuaded her. So all three came over. They walked through the woods and climbed the fence. Their cheeks glowed with the cold when they came in the door. Miss Lacy and Mrs. Steele carried a wicker basket between them.

''Popcorn and cranberries to thread,'' said Miss Lacy.

''And eggnog to drink. My father's recipe. Very powerful,'' said Mrs. Steele with a wink.

When the coats were hung up and the boots were put in front of the radiator, everyone got to work. Miss Lacy sat in the rocker threading three cranberries, five pieces of popcorn, three cranberries, over and over. Mrs. Steele helped Mrs. Mott with the cookies. Lydia and Emily decorated each batch with frosting and sprinkles. Mr. Mott put the lights on the tree, trying to get all the colors spread apart.

Finally, at dusk, it was time to decorate the tree. Mr. Mott lit a fire, and Mrs. Mott put on Christmas music with flutes and bells. Lydia and her aunts joined right in, hanging ornaments that had been in the Mott family for years.

Emily watched everyone trimming the tree together. This feels like we're all one family, she thought. All connected, even though we're not related.

Later, after dinner, they walked to Ivy's for the caroling. It was a cold night with bright moonlight shining on the new snow. About twenty people gathered outside the Adams house. In their down jackets and coats they looked like a pile of colorful pillows clustered together: red, blue, green, purple. Mr. Adams gave everyone a song book, and Mrs. Adams handed out candles stuck through the bottoms of paper cups.

''The bottom of the cup will catch the wax as it drips, and the sides will protect the flame from the wind.''

The carolers walked from house to house, stopping at each door to sing. Emily stood between Ivy and Lydia. She could pick out her parents' voices in the crowd as they sang. She glanced around at the familiar faces, lit by candles in the dark. She felt safe and happy, surrounded this way by friends and family.

Then she noticed that Lydia wasn't really singing. She was biting her lip and she looked sad and worried. She probably misses her parents, Emily thought. I should think of something to cheer her up. Something to do with the dollhouse, maybe.

Emily kept on thinking as they walked and sang. By the time they returned to Ivy's for hot cider, she still hadn't come up with an idea.

But first thing in the morning she thought of a plan.

Her mother helped her with the details at breakfast.

"You have only two days left, so we'll have to hurry," said Mrs. Mott.

Together they made a list: glue, scissors, yarn, buttons, scraps of fabric, Christmas paper, sequins, toothpicks, and more.

"Search the house first," said Mrs. Mott.

They looked in the sewing box and the desk drawers, in the top of the closet and the bottom of the toy box. They searched the drawer in the kitchen, the cabinet in the bathroom, and even in Mr. Mott's toolbox.

Then they went to the variety store. They bought clay and pipe cleaners, rickrack, a packet

of foreign stamps, sequins, and gummed stars—
silver, blue, and red.

When everything was packed, Mrs. Mott tied
a red ribbon around the box and stuck a sprig
of holly through the bow.

"Good luck," she called as Emily walked
down the driveway.

Emily stopped once to break a small bushy
branch off a little evergreen tree and put it in
her pocket.

Miss Lacy opened the door to the Witches'
House. "Oh, you've brought your present over
early. We can put it under the tree."

Emily set the big box down on the floor. "No,
it's for right now. It's a before-Christmas
present."

Lydia poked her head over the banister.
"Come on up. I'm in the attic."

Emily carried the box upstairs and set it
down beside the dollhouse.

"What is it?" asked Lydia.

"Open it up and guess."

Lydia untied the bow and began to unpack
the box. As she pulled out more and more things,
she looked baffled.

"Stars, sequins, erasers, toothpicks. I don't get it! What is all this stuff?"

"You can't guess?" asked Emily.

"No. I give up. Tell me!"

"It's a Christmas kit for the dollhouse people. We're going to make them a Christmas."

Lydia smiled slowly as she got the idea. "We can be their Santa Claus. Giant Santas!"

Emily nodded. "There's enough stuff here to make presents for everyone." She pulled the little evergreen branch out of her pocket. It was just the right size. "And we'll even make them a tree."

"We can use this holly from the top of the box for the front door," Lydia said. "This is going to be fun."

They worked together all afternoon and most of the next day, which was Christmas Eve. Emily used a piece of clay as a stand for the little tree. She and Lydia decorated it with the paper stars, sequins, and red rickrack.

"It looks just right for this family," said Lydia, setting the tree in a corner of the living room.

Next they made presents: tiny books for ev-

eryone, a bicycle made out of pipe cleaners for Martha, a walking stick for Mr. Higgins, a new blanket for the baby, a kite for William, and new music for Mrs. Higgins' piano. Lydia made the cook a new apron and an old-fashioned radio cut out of cardboard.

"She can listen while she cooks."

"I bet this is the best Christmas this family ever had," said Emily, looking over the pile of presents.

"It's probably the *only* Christmas they ever had." Lydia laughed, pleased with her creations.

Carefully the girls wrapped all the presents, using tiny squares of gift wrapping paper and little bits of tape. Then they put the doll family to bed and placed the presents around the tree. When every present was in place, they sat back and enjoyed the scene.

The little house was filled with Christmas. Holly hung from the front door and over the mantel. The tree glittered in the corner, with the gifts in bright paper stacked around it. The dining room table was set for Christmas breakfast. Upstairs the doll people lay in their beds, dreaming.

Lydia sighed happily. "This was more fun than my own Christmas."

Emily looked at her friend's happy face and felt satisfied. Her plan had worked. Lydia hadn't looked sad once during the whole project.

Soon Emily had to go home for dinner. The satisfied feeling lasted all evening.

That night, before she climbed into bed, she looked out the window. She could hear her parents talking downstairs, their voices low and sometimes laughing. Outside, the snow family that she and Lydia had made on the first day of the snowstorm stood in the moonlight. From where Emily was standing, it looked as if the arms of the snow family were touching. It reminded her of the dollhouse family all tucked in their beds. So many families, all close together, she thought.

Then she remembered Lydia's father. She made a wish on the star shining above the house next door. "I hope Lydia's father gets better very fast."

## The Dollhouse Christmas

On Christmas morning the Motts opened their presents and then had pancakes for breakfast. Emily's favorite present was a pair of ice skates with green pom-poms on the toes.

After breakfast she went next door, carrying a loaf of Christmas bread for Lydia's aunts.

Lydia and her aunts were sitting in the sun porch as usual. Their Christmas tree stood in a corner, between the window and the fireplace.

Lydia showed Emily her favorite gift, a box of watercolors and real watercolor paper.

"But my best present came this morning. My mother called. She said my father's feeling better. The medicine is finally starting to work. If he keeps on improving like this, he'll come home right after New Year's. That's when I'm going home, too."

"We're all delighted," said Miss Lacy. "It's the best present we could have asked for, even though we'll miss Lydia when she goes." She gave her niece a hug.

Lydia squirmed a little but looked pleased.

"I'll be back next summer," she said to Emily. "We can be friends then, too."

Emily nodded. "We can take the doll family outside and give them a picnic. They can have adventures, like the Borrowers did."

"Hey! We have to give them their presents," Lydia said. "Come on!"

She raced upstairs with Emily right behind her. They were both singing "Here Comes Santa Claus" in their loudest voices.

# GRANDMA'S PRESENT

It seemed to Emily that it snowed all winter. The snow that started when Lydia was visiting stayed on the ground until January. Then new storms came, one after the other, so the drifts lining the streets stayed high. Winter kept hanging on right into March, even though everyone wished it would leave.

Emily's birthday came in the middle of March, the perfect time for a birthday. Everyone needed cheering up. The children were tired of gray days and snow and mud, tired of boots and mittens and staying inside.

"The end of winter always drags," said Mr. Mott as he leafed through seed catalogs.

"I wish it were spring right now!" said Emily, staring out the window at the muddy front lawn.

Mrs. Mott was planting seeds in starter trays. "It will be spring before you know it. That reminds me, we have to make plans for your birthday. What kind of party do you want?"

"If it were spring, we could have a picnic," Emily said in a grumpy voice.

"And if this were Alaska, we could make an igloo," added her father with a wink.

"Oh, come on," said Mrs. Mott. "We can still have fun. Let's go ice skating at the rink and have a taffy pull. It will be a real winter party."

"Can it be a sleepover?"

"Okay, but no more than five guests," said Mrs. Mott.

Emily thought about whom to invite. Ivy, Phyllis, Mary Louise, Patricia, and who else? Lydia wouldn't be back until summer, and she couldn't invite Leo to a sleepover.

"How about four girls to sleep over and two boys just for the party?" That would be Leo and Johnny.

"Sounds good to me," said Mrs. Mott.

Emily told Ivy about the party the next day in school.

"So what do you want for your birthday?" Ivy asked.

"It's a secret."

"How can a birthday present be a secret? How will you get it if you keep it a secret?"

Emily smiled. "I wished for it."

Ivy was amazed. She never had secrets. She told everybody everything.

"Ivy Yackety-Yak," Leo called her. "And Emily Say-Little-Know-Much." Leo liked to make up funny names and pretend they were Indian names.

"Leo Baloney-Head," Ivy said in return. "Leo Talk-Much-Say-Nothing."

Leo just laughed.

Emily laughed, too, but she didn't tell her secret wish.

"Do you believe in wishes?" she asked her mother one day.

"Sometimes. A little, I guess," her mother said. "They're fun. Like little surprise packages. You never know if they're going to come true, but when they do, it's like getting a present."

"Do you still make wishes?" Emily asked.

"Sure," said her mom. "Don't you?"

Emily nodded.

Her mother continued. "Sometimes I have silly wishes, just daydreams really, like living on an island or inheriting a castle. And other times I have little wishes, like hoping your father will bring home coffee ice cream for dessert tonight." She paused and smiled. "My most important wishes have come true."

"Like what?"

"Well, I wished I'd meet someone with a good sense of humor who liked kids, and I did."

"That was Dad, right?"

"Right. And then I wished I'd have a little girl and she'd be healthy and smart and nice to have around."

"Me?" asked Emily.

"Who else?" Her mother grinned. "Yes, you!"

Emily grinned back, feeling very content, and she kept right on making wishes.

Her secret birthday wish was for a locket like the one in the jewelry store window, a little gold locket with her birthstone set in the center. It was different from anything else she'd ever wanted. It took her by surprise. She didn't know what she'd put inside, but she wanted it very much. She wished for it every night on the evening star, a secret wish.

Plans for the birthday party moved along smoothly. Leo and Johnny agreed to come, even though they'd be the only boys. All the girls accepted the invitations, too. Mrs. Mott made five funny striped nightcaps.

Emily decided on the menu: pizza with sausage and pepperoni, soda, potato chips, vanilla ice cream, and chocolate cake with fudge icing.

"Deadly," said her parents.

"Yum," said Emily.

The party was a big success. The skating rink wasn't very crowded, so they could skate together holding hands.

After skating they ate dinner at Emily's house. Johnny Ringer ate four pieces of pizza.

"Not bad for a short guy, huh?" he said, polishing off the last slice.

"Save some room for dessert," warned Mrs. Mott.

Emily opened her presents after dessert. Ivy gave her a diary.

"Something to write your secrets in," she said.

Leo gave her a chess set.

"I'll teach you how to play," he promised.

Phyllis gave her a big box of Magic Markers. Mary Louise and Patricia gave her a present together. It was a box kite, blue and green and white. Johnny gave her a jigsaw puzzle.

"I know you like to figure things out," he said.

Last of all she opened her parents' present. It was a big box, much too big for a locket. Oh, well, thought Emily, the locket wish didn't work.

She took the wrapping paper off, and inside she found a tennis racket.

"We thought you might like to learn," said Mr. Mott. "You can take lessons at the playground this summer."

Emily swung the racket at an imaginary ball, imitating the tennis players she had seen on the courts by the high school.

"Thanks! This is neat. I didn't even know I wanted this." She gave them both a kiss.

"Maybe I'll take lessons with you this summer," said Ivy.

"Yeah. My father has an old racket in the attic. Maybe I'll sign up, too," said Leo.

Emily was so pleased with her surprise present that she didn't even think of the locket during the taffy pull.

When all the taffy was eaten, Leo and Johnny went home. Mr. Mott built a fire in the living room fireplace, and the girls spread their sleeping bags out on the floor.

"Sleep tight," said Mr. Mott after he had put the screen in front of the fire and turned out the lights. The room was lit softly by the burning logs.

Emily followed her parents out to the hall and gave each of them a hug.

"Happy birthday, birthday girl. Have a good time?" her father asked.

Emily nodded happily. Her mother straightened Emily's nightcap.

"Get everything you wished for?" she asked.

"Just about. And I got some things I didn't wish for but I would have if I'd thought of them."

"Well, don't forget, there's still Grandma's present. She's coming for Sunday dinner, and she's bringing a surprise."

Emily went back to the living room and snuggled into her sleeping bag. She could hear the occasional crackle of the fire. Phyllis was telling a ghost story, but she kept forgetting what happened next, so it wasn't very scary.

"Hey," said Ivy, sitting up. "We forgot to give Emily her birthday spanking."

"Not now! I'm almost asleep," said Emily.

"And I'm too full to move," said Phyllis, holding onto her stomach.

"Okay then. We'll get you in the morning," Ivy promised.

But luckily for Emily, the next morning they forgot.

On Saturday and Sunday Emily played with her presents. She took her chess set over to Leo's, and he tried to teach her how to play. It was hard to remember how each piece moved.

"I'll write down the moves for you on a card, and then you can practice at home," he said.

Emily wrote in her diary, too. On Saturday she described the party and listed her presents. And on Sunday she wrote about her grandmother coming. This made her think of the locket again. Maybe Grandma will guess what I wished for, she thought. Maybe she had a locket when she was little.

But when Grandma Eve arrived on Sunday afternoon, Emily knew right away that the present wasn't a locket. Her grandmother handed her a big box, even bigger than the tennis racket box, but not as heavy. Emily shook it, but nothing rattled. There was a soft thump, thud, as the present inside slid back and forth.

Her grandmother gave her a kiss on the cheek.

''Let's open it in the living room,'' suggested Mrs. Mott. ''Come on, Mother, we can all get comfortable and watch the show.'' She gave her a wink.

Emily knew then that the two of them had planned this surprise together. Whatever was in the box was something they had discussed.

The two of them were so alike. They were both tall and thin, and they had the same easy belly laugh. They're beanpoles like me, Emily thought as she followed them into the living room.

When they were all comfortable, Emily began to unwrap the box. It was covered with white paper, painted all over with little flowers and animals.

''You painted this, didn't you, Grandma?'' said Emily, taking care not to rip the paper.

Then she opened the box. Inside lay a big rag doll, more than two feet tall. She was soft and floppy, with arms and legs that could swing back and forth. Her face was lively, with black button eyes and an embroidered mischievous smile. She didn't have the flat, dumb expression that so many rag dolls have.

Her hair was made of soft brown wool, parted in the middle and braided down her back. On her feet were black high-button shoes made of cloth.

She wasn't a baby doll or even a little girl. She was older, almost a young woman.

Emily looked at her and blinked. A rag doll! Emily stared at it in disbelief. What could Grandma be thinking? Does she think that I'm still a baby?

Her grandmother saw immediately that Emily didn't like the doll. Her mother saw it, too. She reached forward and lifted the doll out of the box, holding it in front of her.

"What a beautiful piece of work," said Mrs. Mott. "You must have been sewing all winter. She's lovely. A real family treasure."

Grandma looked at the doll lovingly. "I've gotten rather fond of her while I've been working on her. I had such fun designing the clothes. She's right in style with all those country skirts they're showing."

Emily kept quiet. She didn't know what to say. She didn't want the doll. She couldn't even see that it was beautiful.

Her grandmother looked over at her with a gentle, thoughtful expression. "Looks like I made a mistake. I thought you'd like her. She looks like a doll I had when I was little. Sarah, I called her. She sat on my bed, and I kept her even after high school."

Grandma picked up the doll and fluffed out her skirt. "It sounds silly, but I guess I thought of Sarah as a friend. I used to talk to her. I kept her on my bed until I married. Then I packed her away for my own little girl. Your Aunt Pat still has her. She's going to give her to your cousin Annie, I think. So I thought you might like a Sarah doll, too, and you could keep her and maybe pass her on to your own little girl if you have one."

Grandma smoothed the hair on the doll and gazed at her face. "She's got an intelligent face, I think."

Then she looked over at Emily again. "I guessed wrong. You're either too old for her or not old enough. I'll save her for someone younger, and pick you out something you'll really like."

She put the doll back in the box.

Emily watched silently. She couldn't pretend she liked the doll. But she hated to hurt her grandmother's feelings.

"I'm sorry, Grandma," she said, not really knowing why she felt sorry.

"I am too, sweetheart," said her grandmother. "I should've known better."

Emily's mother didn't say anything until dinner was over and Grandmother had gone home, carrying the big box under her arm.

"She worked on that doll for a long time, Emily."

"I know, Mom, but I don't even play with dolls anymore. Doesn't she know that I'm not a baby now?"

"I don't think she expected you to play with it the same way you would if you were younger. I think she wanted you to have something she had made for you. Something that reminded her of her own childhood. It would be a link between the two of you. But I guess you can't understand that yet.''

Emily didn't answer. She felt like crying, but she wasn't sure why.

All week long Emily thought about the doll. She was a young lady, she remembered, almost old enough to go to dances. The more she thought about the doll, the more she wanted her. She remembered her face, and the blue apron with the little tucked pocket. That doll would fit nicely on her bed, leaning up against the headboard. There was something comforting about the idea of pretending a doll was your friend and talking to it when you needed to. You could tell secrets to a doll like the Sarah doll. Even secret wishes.

But it was too late now. Grandma had taken the doll back to her house. She was going to give it to one of the younger cousins. Maybe to that horrible whiny Dorothy.

Emily wished she could turn back time and have her birthday all over again. Then when she opened the box and saw the doll, she'd be pleased. ''Oh, thanks, Grandma!'' she'd say, and she'd give that doll a big hug.

But she couldn't turn back time.

On Saturday Mrs. Mott said, "Grandma's coming over later with your birthday present. So stick around in the afternoon, okay?"

Emily waited on the front porch, trying to decide what to do. She didn't want a new present. She wanted the Sarah doll.

Finally she heard Grandma's old car driving up the street. She heard the car door slam and her grandmother's footsteps coming up the gravel walk. Her grandmother's hands were stuffed into her windbreaker pockets. No sign of a box or present.

Grandma sat down on the step beside Emily and rubbed her palms on the knees of her corduroy pants. "Ready for a late present?" she asked with a grin.

Emily tried to smile back, but it came out crooked.

"What's the matter?" asked Grandma.

Emily rested her head against her grandmother's shoulder.

"Gran, did you give away the doll yet?"

"No, not yet. Why?"

Emily paused before she answered. "I really want her."

Grandma took one of Emily's hands and held it in her own warm hand. "You don't have to pretend for me. My feelings were hurt only for a minute. Not everybody likes dolls, that's all."

But Emily wasn't pretending. "No, Grandma, I really do want her. She's the only present I want. I thought about her all week."

"Are you sure? Sure you're sure?"

"Yes! I'm absolutely sure. I'm going to call her Sarah, and I'll keep her forever, and when I'm older I can tell my children that my grandmother made her. Please? Please can I have her?"

"Please may I have her," Grandma corrected automatically. "If you're absolutely sure you want her, yes, you may. I made her especially for you. Probably because you remind me so much of myself when I was your age."

She patted Emily's knee. "But I do have another present here in my pocket, and I don't know what to do with this one. Do you think there's any rule against giving someone two presents for one birthday?''

Emily smiled and shook her head.

''Good, because I don't know what else to do with this except give it to someone with a March birthday.''

She reached into her pocket and pulled out a tiny box. It was painted all over like a little house, with a door, windows, shutters, and even tiny window boxes.

Emily lifted the cover and looked under the piece of cotton that lay like a little blanket over the inside. When she saw what was there, she gasped.

''Grandma, how did you know?''

''Know what?''

''Know what I wished for. A locket!''

Her grandmother smiled, her eyes crinkling up at the corners. ''Is it really what you wished for?''

''Yes! Exactly. A locket with my birthstone on it.''

''Open it up and look inside.''

Emily pushed the tiny clasp, and the locket

sprang open. Inside, in the little frames, were a tiny photo of her mother on one side and her father on the other.

"When you get older, you'll probably have other pictures you'll want to put in it."

Emily grinned. She liked being teased about getting older.

"Grandma, how did you know that I wanted this?"

"Just a lucky guess. Maybe it's because we're so much alike. I just thought this was something you'd want."

She helped Emily put the locket around her neck.

"Let's go in and show your mother. Then we can pick up the doll at my house and stop for ice cream on the way home."

Emily gave her grandmother the biggest hug she could. Then they went inside.

Mrs. Mott decided to come along for ice cream, too. They went to Mahoney's, across from the railroad station.

Emily leaned her elbows on the cool marble counter and tucked her feet around the legs of the wrought-iron stool. When the waiter came, she ordered a butterscotch sundae. Her mother and grandmother ordered hot fudge.

Waiting for the ice cream, Emily looked in the mirror behind the counter. She stared back at herself, sitting between her mother and her grandmother.

We look alike, she noticed again. Thin faces, blue eyes, straight hair, blond on me and Mom, white on Gran.

She smiled at herself, tucked in between them, connected.

She thought of all the other people she was connected to. Ivy and Leo, The Lucky Stones. Johnny Ringer. Lydia and the dollhouse people. Mrs. Steele and Miss Lacy.

The mirror reflected the other people in the shop, too, all sitting at tables eating ice cream. An old couple by the window, a family with three little kids, a boy and a girl holding hands in the corner, a man with a beard sitting alone, two ladies with fancy braided hair.

They're all connected to other people, too. Everybody is, somehow, Emily thought. That's

what's been nice about this year. Making friends. I didn't even wish for them, either. They just happened.

Emily's spoon clinked against the bottom of her sundae dish. She had finished her ice cream without even noticing. All that was left was the cherry she always saved for last. She scraped the last drops of ice cream from the dish and popped the cherry into her mouth.

CHRISTINE MCDONNELL graduated from Barnard College and Columbia University School of Library Service. She has worked as a teacher and children's librarian, as well as a writer of children's books. She currently teaches at the Pierce School in Brookline, Massachusetts. She lives with her family in Boston.

DIANE DE GROAT is the illustrator of many books for children, including *Chasing Trouble* (Viking) and *Toad Food & Measle Soup,* by Christine McDonnell (Puffin). She received her Bachelor of Fine Arts degree from Pratt Institute. Ms. de Groat lives in Yonkers, New York, with her husband and daughter.